Mouse Loves School

by Lauren Thompson
illustrated by Buket Erdogan

Ready-to-Read

Simon Spotlight

New York   London   Toronto   Sydney

To Charlotte —L. T.

To my heart, my daughter Yagmur —B. E.

SIMON SPOTLIGHT
An imprint of Simon & Schuster Children's Publishing Division
1230 Avenue of the Americas, New York, New York 10020
Text copyright © 2003, 2011 by Lauren Thompson
Illustrations copyright © 2003 by Buket Erdogan
All rights reserved, including the right of reproduction in whole or in part in
any form. SIMON SPOTLIGHT, READY-TO-READ, and colophon are registered
trademarks of Simon & Schuster, Inc. For information about special discounts for
bulk purchases, please contact Simon & Schuster Special Sales at 1-866-506-1949 or
business@simonandschuster.com.
Manufactured in the United States of America 0511 LAK
First Edition 10 9 8 7 6 5 4 3 2 1
Cataloging-in-Publication Data for this title is available from the Library of Congress.
ISBN 978-1-4424-2898-0 (pbk)
ISBN 978-1-4424-2899-7 (hc)

This book was previously pubished, with slightly different text,
as *Mouse's First Day Of School.*

What is this?

Mouse climbs inside.

Mouse climbs out.
He is in a
brand-new place!

Mouse looks around.
Mouse finds four
blocks!

Mouse finds
a red car.

Vrim,

vrum,

vroom!

Mouse finds
a drum.

Thump,

boom,

bump!

Mouse looks up high.

Mouse finds a book!

A, B, C, D!

Mouse finds a
green plant.

Mouse climbs
on the plant.
This is fun!

Mouse finds a table.

Mouse finds paint!

Red, yellow, and blue.
Mouse loves to paint!

Mouse finds crayons.

Mouse draws yellow lines.

Mouse draws yellow dots.

Mouse finds juice.
Mouse finds fruit
and cookies.

It is snack time!

Sip, slurp, crunch!

Mouse finds a puzzle.
Where do the
pieces go?

Triangle, circle, square.
Mouse loves shapes!

Then Mouse finds
his favorite thing.

Mouse finds friends!

Mouse loves friends.

Mouse loves school!